W9-BKO-244
SU SU
GABBY
TIMOTHY
COMPUTER DIGEST
GATOR
FLEX
HENRIETTA

THE E-MAIL MYSTERY

A Golden Book • New York

Western Publishing Company, Inc., Racine, Wisconsin 53404

A Mercer Mayer Ltd./J. R. Sansevere Book

Library of Congress Catalog Card Number: 94-73091
ISBN: 0-307-16181-1/ISBN: 0-307-66181-4 (lib. bdg.) A MCMXCV

Written by Erica Farber/J. R. Sansevere

CRITTER DUDES
LC
VELVET
LITTLE SIST

CRITTER POWER
HIP HOP
KOOL BEAR
WIPE OUT
TIGER
KOOL BEAR
SLICK RICK

CHAPTER 1

A MESSAGE FROM KERNEL KRUNCH

LC peeked into the living room. The coast was clear. He brought his cereal bowl and clicked on the TV. *Kayne's Countdown* on CTV had just started. Kayne hosted all the coolest shows on CTV.

"You're not supposed to be watching TV before school," said Little Sister as she walked into the living room. "I'm telling."

"I'm watching the news," said LC.

"That's not the news," said Little Sister. "It's CTV."

KAYNE: *And we'll be right back after this message from Kernel Krunch.*

LC kept staring at the TV.

KERNEL KRUNCH: *Have you had your Kernel Krunch cereal today?*

LC put a big spoonful of cereal in his mouth and began to chew.

KERNEL KRUNCH: *Well, you should have because YOU could be the winner of my Super Snazzy Krunchometer Watch! That's right. Somewhere out there is a Kernel Krunch box with my watch in it—and it's yours if you can find it!*

Suddenly there was a loud boom and the Kernel's tank shot Kernel Krunch cereal everywhere.

KERNEL KRUNCH: *So start crunching, Kernel Krunch lovers . . . and maybe YOU'll be the lucky winner!*

LC jumped up. "Hey, I'm eating Kernel Krunch cereal," he said, "and I didn't check the box."

When LC ran into the kitchen, he couldn't believe his eyes. There was Little Sister shaking the empty cereal box upside down. Bowls of Kernel Krunch cereal were all over the table.

"No watch in this box," said Little Sister.

"Oh, my," said Mrs. Critter, walking into the kitchen. "Little Sister, what are you doing with all of that cereal?"

"I was hungry," said Little Sister.

"No, you weren't," said LC. "You were looking for the Super Snazzy Krunchometer Watch."

"And you were watching CTV," said Little Sister, sticking her tongue out at LC.

"That's enough," said Mrs. Critter. "Now, Little Sister, put whatever you're not eating back in the box."

Just then Mr. Critter walked in. "Now, kids, about this weekend . . . Oh, I'll have some of that Kernel Krunch cereal," he said, taking a bowl and then pouring himself a cup of coffee. "As I was saying, you know your grandmother is getting older, so I want both of you to be extra good this weekend."

"Okay, Dad," said LC. "No problem!"

"Come home right after school," said Mrs. Critter. "Your father and I are leaving as soon as your grandmother gets here."

Mr. and Mrs. Critter were going away for the weekend to celebrate their anniversary at the same romantic cabin in the woods they had gone to for their honeymoon.

LC picked up his knapsack and opened the door. "See ya later," he said.

LC spotted his friends Gabby and Tiger halfway down the block. He ran to catch up with them. Gabby had lived next door to LC ever since he could remember, and Tiger was LC's best friend.

"Hey, guys," called LC. "Wait up."

"You're late," said Gabby, staring at her watch. "Exactly one minute and twenty-three seconds late."

"Sorry," said LC.

"Well, I want to be on time for computer lab," continued Gabby. "Remember Mr. Hogwash said we're going to do something really fun today."

"I bet if I had that Kernel Krunch Super Snazzy Krunchometer Watch, I'd always be on time," said LC.

"That watch is great!" said Tiger.

"Totally," said LC.

CHAPTER 2

CODE NAME: LC

When LC, Tiger, and Gabby got to school, they went right to the computer lab. The rest of the Critter Kids were already there, sitting in front of their terminals.

"Okay, class, it's time for you to turn on your computers," said Mr. Hogwash. "Today we are going on-line. Does anybody happen to know what *on-line* means?"

"Being on-line is like being on a telephone line, only in our case we get on a computer line," said Timothy. "That way we can chat or send messages back and forth, with other computer users in 'real' time." Timothy was the class brain. He once built a radio out of crystals he grew himself.

"Correct," said Mr. Hogwash. "Which means that what you type appears on different computer screens as you type it, provided the other users are all hooked into Critterville On-line."

"Wow!" said Gabby. "That sounds like fun. It's like having computer pen pals."

"But, before we go any further, you all need to select a code name," explained Mr. Hogwash. "It will be the special name by which the computer recognizes you."

"My code name's going to be Nancy Critter," said Gabby, "after my favorite detective."

"Oh, brother," said LC.

"Well, what's your name gonna be?" Gabby asked.

LC thought for a minute. "I don't know," he finally said. "LC, I guess."

"You can't use your real name," said Gabby.

"Why not?" asked LC. "I like my name."

"Okay, class, log on and let's get started," said Mr. Hogwash.

After LC logged on, he stared at the computer. Suddenly messages appeared on his screen:

—Nancy Critter: Has anyone read *The Alphabet Soup Mystery*?

—Agatha Critter: Yes, (((it's my favorite book))) !!! (^_^).

LC tried to think of something clever to type. All of a sudden a symbol in the shape of an envelope flashed in the corner of his screen.

"Hey, Gabby," said LC. "What's this envelope thing on my computer?"

Gabby went over to LC's computer. "Beats me," she said when she saw the envelope symbol. "Hey, Timothy," she called, "come over here and look at this weird thing on LC's computer."

Timothy walked over to LC's computer.

"What's going on, dude?" asked Tiger from his computer terminal. The rest of the Critter Kids turned and stared at LC.

"Someone sent LC a message," Timothy announced. Then he turned to LC. "All you have to do is click twice on that envelope symbol and you will receive the electronic mail, or E-mail, that another user sent you."

LC clicked twice on the envelope symbol and this message appeared on the screen:

—Kernel Krunch will arrive at 16 Green Frog Lane tomorrow at 1000 hours.

"Hey, that's my house!" said LC in surprise. "Do you think I won the Super Snazzy Krunchometer Watch?!"

"No," said Gabby. "You have to find it, remember? It's in a box of cereal."

The Critter Kids gathered around LC's computer. They all stared at the strange message.

Nobody could figure out what it meant or who might have sent it.

"We have to get to the bottom of this," said Gabby. "It's our first high-tech mystery!"

LC groaned. Gabby was always looking for mysteries. And they usually meant only one thing for LC—trouble.

"Mr. Critter," said Mr. Hogwash, "is there some special reason why you have gathered the entire class around your computer?"

"Uh . . . no," said LC as the Critter Kids scooted quickly back to their seats.

At the same time on the other side of Critterville, in an old abandoned warehouse, another computer user had also received LC's mysterious message.

"Good job, Jellybean!" said Lulu Creamcheese with an evil laugh as she stared at her computer screen. She dropped a sardine in her mouth and swallowed it whole. "When my trusty assistant, Jellybean, returns we'll just have to take a little trip to 16 Green Frog Lane . . ."

TO BE DELIVERED...

Later that afternoon when LC got home from school, he helped his dad pack the luggage in the car.

"Now, LC, don't forget to turn on the new sprinkler system at night," said Mr. Critter, putting another suitcase in the trunk.

"No problem, Dad," said LC.

Just then Mrs. Crabtree, the Critters' neighbor, walked down her front steps to her shiny blue car that was parked right in front of her house.

"Good afternoon, Eugenia!" Mr. Critter called across the street to Mrs. Crabtree. "Nice wax job."

Mrs. Crabtree waved her feather duster at Mr. Critter. "Thank you," she said as she began to dust the front fender of her car. "I just had it done with that special hot wax treatment. It's supposed to keep the car shiny all year long. Like I always say, 'A clean car is like a clean mind—it can never be clean enough.'"

LC rolled his eyes. Mrs. Crabtree was always saying corny stuff like that.

Mr. Critter slammed the trunk of the car closed. "Okay," he called to Mrs. Critter. "We're ready to go!"

Grandma, Mrs. Critter, and Little Sister walked out of the house.

"The emergency numbers are next to the phone in the kitchen," said Mrs. Critter, getting into the car. "And Little Sister's allergy medicine is in the bathroom cabinet," she added. "And . . ."

"Have a good trip!" said Grandma.

"Don't forget to get me a present!" said Little Sister.

"Oh, I almost forgot," said Mr. Critter, sticking his head out of the car window. "I'm expecting a package from the lab tomorrow morning. Just leave it with the mail."

"Is it your chip, Dad?" asked LC.

Mr. Critter was an engineer at Coconut Computers, the biggest computer company in Critterville. He had been working on a top-secret computer chip.

"Yup," said Mr. Critter. "This chip is going to mean my next promotion."

"My son, the computer genius," said Grandma with a big smile. "Now, you kids better get going. That second honeymoon won't wait, you know."

LC, Little Sister, and Grandma waved good-bye as Mr. and Mrs. Critter drove away. When the car turned the corner and was out of sight, Grandma suddenly pulled off her apron.

"All right, kids," said Grandma, high-fiving first LC and then Little Sister. "It's time to par-ty! Invite your friends over. We're going to order pizza!"

"Yay!" shouted LC and Little Sister.

The three of them went into the house, just as a big red car came driving slowly down Green Frog Lane.

"That white house is number fifteen," said Lulu Creamcheese, staring at Mrs. Crabtree's house. Then she pointed to the Critters' mailbox. "There it is—16 Green Frog Lane."

"Should I pull into the driveway?" asked Jellybean.

"A brilliant idea," snapped Lulu. "You sloopering shnook! We'll just tell these Critters we're waiting to steal their package. Pull across the street so we can keep an eye on the house."

Nobody noticed the red car except Mrs. Crabtree. She thought nothing of it except that it was parked awfully close to her newly waxed car.

CHAPTER 4

OFF THE HOOK...

When LC woke up the next morning, he smelled something delicious. Yo Yo's nose began to twitch as he got a whiff of the smell, too.

"Let's go, Yo Yo!" said LC to his dog. "Grandma's making something great for breakfast."

LC slid down the banister as Yo Yo barked and ran down the stairs. Little Sister was on the phone in the hallway.

"What are you doing?" asked LC.

Little Sister put one hand on the mouthpiece of the phone.

"Just ordering some things we need from the market," she said.

"Well, I'm gonna go eat breakfast," said LC.

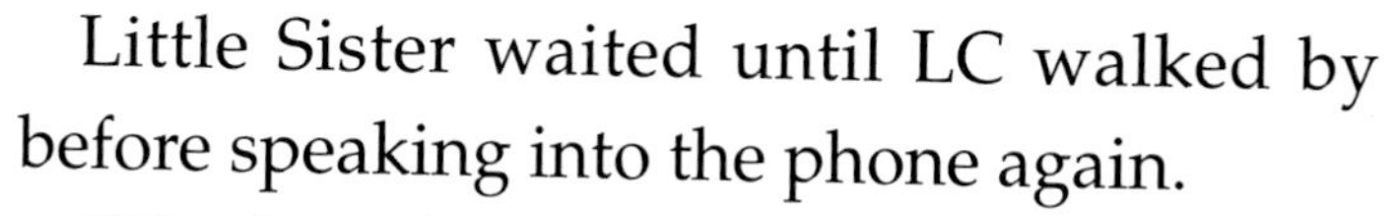

Little Sister waited until LC walked by before speaking into the phone again.

"That's right," whispered Little Sister. "I said two hundred boxes."

LC and Yo Yo walked into the kitchen.

"Good morning, LC!" said Grandma, who was at the stove flipping pancakes. She handed him a big plateful.

"Thanks, Grandma," said LC, sitting down. "They smell great!"

"Where's Little Sister?" asked Grandma.

"Here I am, Grandma," said Little Sister,

walking into the kitchen.

"Now eat up, everybody," Grandma said. She put a plate of pancakes in front of Little Sister. "We're going bowling and then to see the new Schwarzecritter movie. It opens today and I want to get there early so we get good seats."

"Cool!" said LC. Arnold Schwarzecritter was LC's favorite action adventure hero.

"Can Bunny come?" asked Little Sister.

"Why, of course, dearie," said Grandma. "LC, you can invite your friends, too."

Just then the phone rang. "I'll get it," said LC, grabbing the phone. "Yo," he said.

"Excuse me, is this Critterville 9-3919?" shouted Mrs. Critter from a phone booth by a very noisy highway.

LC could barely hear the voice.

"Maybe," said LC. His parents had always told him to be careful about giving information to strangers.

"Helloooo!" yelled Mrs. Critter as a big truck roared by. "Is anybody there?"

"Who's on the phone?" asked Grandma.

"I don't know," said LC. "There's all this noise. Sounds like a crank call to me."

"Then hang up, dear," said Grandma. "And we just won't answer the phone for a while in case they try to call back."

LC shrugged and hung up the phone.

A few seconds later it rang again. LC, Little Sister, and Grandma didn't answer it. They just let it ring.

Meanwhile Mrs. Critter was getting frantic. "I think we should go back," she said to Mr. Critter. "Something's wrong! No one's answering the phone."

"Maybe they're out," said Mr. Critter.

"I don't think so," said Mrs. Critter. "Someone answered the phone the first time I called. He sounded very strange. Something is wrong."

"Stop worrying," said Mr. Critter. "I'm sure everything's okay."

"I don't know," said Mrs. Critter. "I think I better call again."

The phone kept ringing and ringing. Finally Grandma got so fed up she took the phone off the hook. "There," she said. "That'll fix that crank caller."

Later that morning Bunny and the Critter Kids all came over to the Critters' house.

"It's really cool that your grandmother likes Schwarzecritter," said Tiger.

"Yeah," said Gator.

"I love going to the movies," said Henrietta, chewing on a big jelly doughnut. "They have the best popcorn."

"Okay, kids, let's go," said Grandma. "We have a big day ahead of us."

The Critter Kids hopped into the back of Grandma's new Critter Cruiser van. Little Sister and Bunny sat in front. Nobody noticed the big red car that was parked across the street. Lulu and Jellybean watched Grandma and the Critter Kids from inside it.

"Everyone buckle up!" said Grandma.

Just then a Critter Express truck pulled up and a delivery critter jumped out. He ran over to the van with a package.

"Critter Express for a Mr. Critter," said the delivery critter.

"Oh, that package is for my son," said Grandma. "I'll take it."

The delivery critter handed Grandma a box of Kernel Krunch cereal.

"Are you sure this is the right package?" asked Grandma.

"Yes, ma'am," said the delivery critter.

"It's from the Coconut Computer lab."

"How strange," said Grandma. She took the box and put it in her bag.

"Wait a minute," said Gabby. "Remember what your E-mail said."

"Yeah," said LC. "It said Kernel Krunch would be at my house at ten o'clock."

"Right," said Gabby. "And do you know what time it is now?" She held out her watch to show the Critter Kids the time. "It's exactly ten o'clock."

"I bet it's just a coincidence," said Henrietta.

"No," said Gabby. "This is our second clue. We've got to get to the bottom of this E-mail mystery."

Meanwhile Lulu Creamcheese was fuming as she watched Grandma's van drive down Green Frog Lane.

"Drats," said Lulu. "That old bag got the package. Those computer nerds think they're so funny. They put the chip in a box of Kernel Krunch cereal."

"I don't get it," said Jellybean, shifting the car into REVERSE.

"The chip is called Kernel Krunch," said Lulu. "Remember? It takes huge amounts of numerical data and 'crunches' it so that millions of numbers fit on one tiny chip."

"Oh, yeah," said Jellybean. "That's funny."

"Quiet, pea brain!" said Lulu. "That chip is worth billions of dollars on the black market. And it's going to be mine, all mine! Just make sure you don't lose that Critter Cruiser. Now, step on it!"

Jellybean stepped on the gas. Suddenly there was a loud bang. Jellybean had

backed right into Mrs. Crabtree's car. There was a big dent in her shiny silver fender.

"You big dum-dum!" screamed Lulu.

Jellybean shifted the gear to DRIVE and squealed away just as Mrs. Crabtree looked out the window. Mrs. Crabtree couldn't believe her eyes. Before she could even open her front door, Lulu and Jellybean had disappeared down the block in a cloud of smoke.

CHAPTER 5

PASS THE NACHOS!

Grandma and the Critter Kids bowled three games and then headed over to the Critterville Cinema. While they were busy getting some snacks and finding seats in the crowded theater, Lulu and Jellybean were trying to find a parking space.

"These are the best seats," said Little Sister as she plopped down next to Grandma.

"Yeah," said Bunny, taking a seat on the other side of Grandma. "I love sitting in the front row."

"Hey, Bunny," said LC, leaning over. "Tell Little Sister to pass the nachos."

"LC wants you to pass the nachos," Bunny said to Little Sister.

"No way," said Little Sister, holding on tightly to an order of gooey cheese nachos. "Not until the movie starts."

"How 'bout passing us some of those nachos," shouted Tiger from his seat.

"Ooh, gross!" said Velvet. "Those things aren't even made with real cheese. It's cheese-flavored glue!"

"I love them," said Henrietta, shoving a handful of popcorn into her mouth.

Just then Lulu and Jellybean walked into the theater.

"There they are," said Lulu, peering over her dark sunglasses. "They're sitting in the front row. Let's go!"

"Don't you think that's too close to watch the movie?" asked Jellybean. "They say it's really bad for your eyes."

"You bingo brain!" said Lulu. "We're not here to watch the stupid movie! We're here to get the package. Anyway, I hate these movies. The good guys always win."

The lights went down just as Lulu and Jellybean slid into the two seats next to Little Sister.

"Who's that?" asked Velvet as a character swimming underwater in scuba gear appeared on the screen.

"That's Arnold Schwarzecritter," said Henrietta.

At that moment Arnold Schwarzecritter hacked a huge hole in the ice above him with an ice pick and pulled himself out of the water. Then he slipped out of his scuba suit. Underneath it he was wearing a black tuxedo.

"Cool!" said Tiger.

"Oooooh," said Grandma. "Isn't Arnold Schwarzecritter dreamy?"

Little Sister and Bunny looked at each other and giggled.

"Can you pass the nachos now?" LC called to Little Sister.

"Hold your horses," said Little Sister, taking a big bite.

"Hey, Little Sister, how about sharing

some of those nachos?" asked Gabby.

"Why don't you and LC move down a seat closer to me?" Grandma said to Gabby. "That way you two can have some nachos, too."

While LC and Gabby were switching seats, Grandma's bag accidentally got kicked closer to Lulu.

"Perfect," said Lulu, eyeing the bag. She

bent down and reached slowly toward it.

"Let me have the nachos," said LC.

"Uh-uh," said Little Sister, eating another nacho. "I'm not done yet."

Lulu's hand moved even closer to the bag. Just as LC was about to grab the nachos there was a huge explosion in the movie. Little Sister jumped out of her seat.

The nachos flew up in the air and landed right on Lulu's head. There was gooey cheese all over Lulu. Jellybean snickered.

"Oh, my goodness!" exclaimed Grandma, reaching for her bag and pulling out some tissues. Then she leaned over and handed them to Lulu. "I'm Harriet Critter," she called over to Lulu. "Sorry about the mess."

"Lulu Creamcheese is my name," said Lulu, gritting her teeth. She wiped some cheese off her nose. "It's nothing."

"Lulu Creamcheese—what a strange name," Gabby whispered to LC. "Hey, wait a minute. Her initials are LC. Just like in your E-mail."

"So?" said LC. His eyes were glued to the screen, where Arnold and his pals were making their getaway in a big white van.

"The pieces of the puzzle are coming together," said Gabby in an excited voice. "First the package and now this. You can't tell me it's just a coincidence that she has the same exact initials."

"Yes, I can," said LC. "And now if you'll leave me alone, I'd like to watch the movie."

Lulu stared at Grandma, who held her bag securely on her lap. "Drats and double drats," said Lulu. "Now we'll have to watch the rest of this stupid film. But when it's over, I'm going to get that package no matter what . . ."

CHAPTER 6

THE GETAWAY

"Well, all I have to say is Schwarzecritter is my kind of critter," said Grandma as she and the Kids drove out of the theater parking lot.

"He's one cool dude," said Tiger.

"I love his accent," Velvet said. "It's very romantic."

"His chase scenes are the best," said Gator.

"Yeah, like when he was being followed by the big red car," added Henrietta.

"Just like the big red car that's following us now," said Gabby, looking out the back window of the van.

"That car's not following us," said LC. "You're letting your imagination run away with you again."

"Who's following us?" asked Grandma, winking at LC in the rearview mirror.

"A big red car," said Gabby. "It's two cars behind us."

"Well, we'll just have to lose them," said Grandma as she put on her blinker and changed lanes.

LC stared out the back window. He watched as the red car also changed lanes. That's strange, LC thought.

"That red car is still with us," said Gabby.

Just then Grandma made a sharp right.

Lulu hit the dashboard with her fist. "Don't lose them!" she shouted at Jellybean. "Step on it, now!"

Jellybean swerved to the right and just barely made the turn. Both vehicles approached a traffic light.

Grandma drove through the intersection as the light changed from green to yellow. Jellybean stepped on the gas as the light turned red. Suddenly a police siren sounded. A motorcycle came roaring down the road.

"You idiot!!!" shouted Lulu.

"Do you want me to lose him, boss?" asked Jellybean.

"Just pull over and get the ticket," said Lulu. "You've been watching too many Schwarzecritter movies. I'll handle this."

Jellybean pulled over to the side of the road. The cop got off his motorcycle, walked up to the car, and peered into Jellybean's window. Jellybean gulped.

"Good evening, Officer," said Lulu.

"Sergeant Pokey's the name," said the officer to Jellybean. "I'd like to see your driver's license and car registration."

"Beautiful weather we're having, Sergeant," said Lulu as Jellybean searched his pockets for his wallet. He pulled out a pack of gum, two marbles, and a slingshot—but no driver's license.

"I can't seem to find it," he said. "I must have left my license at home."

"Would you both please step out of the car," said Sergeant Pokey.

Lulu and Jellybean got out of the car.

"Now, which one of you does this car

belong to?" asked Sergeant Pokey.

"It's his," said Lulu at the same moment that Jellybean said, "It's hers."

"Let me ask the question another way," continued Sergeant Pokey. "Do either of you know who owns this car?"

"It's mine!" shouted Lulu and Jellybean at the same time.

"All right then, I'll make the tickets out to both of you," said Sergeant Pokey.

"What?!" shouted Lulu.

"That's right, ma'am," said Sergeant Pokey. "That'll be $100 for running a red light. Another $100 for doing 55 in a 25-mile-an-hour zone. $50 for a broken taillight and $25 each for not wearing your seat belts. The total comes to $300."

"You can't be serious!" shouted Lulu, jumping up

and down and waving her arms in the air.

"Oh, and another $150 for disorderly conduct," said Sergeant Pokey, filling out another ticket.

Sergeant Pokey handed Lulu all the tickets.

"Have a good evening, ma'am," said Sergeant Pokey as he got back on his motorcycle and sped off.

"Now what, boss?" asked Jellybean.

"Those critters are really getting under my skin," said Lulu. "This is it! We're going to get that package before the night is over."

Meanwhile Grandma and the Kids were on their way home from the Critter Cone, where they had gone for ice cream.

"Pretty cool driving, Grandma," said Tiger, taking a big bite of his banana split.

"Why, thank you,

Tiger," said Grandma as she turned onto Green Frog Lane.

"Yeah," said Gabby, taking a sip of her ice cream soda. "You did a great job of losing that red car."

"But it's not like that car was really following us," said LC.

"Oh, yeah?" said Gabby, staring out the back window. "If that red car wasn't following us, then what's it doing parked right across the street from your house?"

CHIP-IN-THE-BOX

Grandma pulled into the driveway.

"What about the red car?" asked Gabby. "Are we going to call the police or the CBI?"

"The CBI?" asked Tiger.

"You know," said Henrietta. "The Critter Bureau of Investigation."

"Don't be silly," said Grandma. "There are lots of red cars just like that one all over Critterville."

"But still," said Gabby. "You have to admit it's kinda strange."

"No, we don't," said LC. "It's nothing."

"Well, I know what I'm going to do," said Grandma, opening the front door. "I'm going to take a nice hot bath."

"Let's watch some TV," said Tiger, walking into the living room.

"Yeah," said Gator. "The Critterville Sonics game is on."

"Good idea," said LC. "But first I've got to turn on the sprinklers out back."

"I'll do that, LC," said Little Sister.

"You will?" said LC.

"Sure," said Little Sister with a big smile. "I always like to help my big brother. Come on, Bunny."

"Are you sure you feel okay?" asked LC, staring at Little Sister.

"Isn't that nice," said Grandma.

Little Sister and Bunny went into the kitchen. Little Sister opened the back door and peered outside. Then she motioned for Bunny to follow her.

"Close the door behind you," whispered Little Sister.

Bunny closed the door. "What's in all those bags?" she asked, pointing to all the grocery bags piled around the back door.

"Boxes of Kernel Krunch cereal," said Little Sister. "And I just know the Super Snazzy Krunchometer Watch is in one of these boxes."

"Wow!" said Bunny.

"Is the coast clear?" asked Little Sister.

"Your grandmother just walked into the kitchen," said Bunny, peeking inside.

"Then we'll have to wait to bring this stuff in," said Little Sister.

Inside, Grandma took the box of Kernel Krunch cereal out of her bag and put it on the counter with the rest of the mail. She looked at the box and shrugged. "Those computer hackers certainly have an odd sense of humor," she said to herself. "Imagine putting a computer chip in a cereal box." Then she left the kitchen.

"The coast's clear," Bunny whispered to Little Sister.

"Okay," said Little Sister. "Let's go."

Across the street under the cover of darkness, Lulu was looking into the Critters' kitchen through her binoculars.

"The Kernel is in the kitchen," said Lulu to Jellybean. "Let's go."

Lulu and Jellybean got out of their car. Jellybean slammed his door shut.

"Be quiet," whispered Lulu.

The sound of the car door slamming woke Mrs. Crabtree. She hopped up and ran to the window. Her eyes opened wide when she saw the red car.

"Ah-ha!" Mrs. Crabtree said. "Whoever hit my car is in for it now!" She picked up her telephone and began to dial.

Meanwhile Little Sister and Bunny were busily bringing box after box of Kernel Krunch cereal into the kitchen. Boxes almost filled the whole room.

At the same time LC and the Critter Kids were watching the basketball game on TV.

"How can you just sit there and watch

TV when we're in the middle of a big mystery?" asked Gabby, standing in front of the TV.

"Yeah," said Velvet.

"Quit blocking the TV," said Tiger. "Hakeem Critter just made another three pointer."

"So what!" said Gabby. "We've got to find out who is in that red car and exactly what they're up to. Anybody with me?"

"I am," said Velvet.

"Anybody else?" asked Gabby, staring at Henrietta and the boys.

"All right," said LC. "Let's go check it out. Then will you let us watch the basketball game in peace?"

Gabby nodded as everybody got up. They followed her out the front door.

Just then they spotted two shadowy figures running across the front lawn toward the back of the house.

"Who was that?" asked Tiger. "And what are they doing in your yard?"

"I told you there was something suspicious going on," said Gabby.

"Maybe you were right!" said LC.

"Now what are we going to do?" asked Henrietta.

"We've got to find out what they're up to," said Gabby. "I just know it has something to do with LC's E-mail message about Kernel Krunch."

"Let's go around the house the other way

so they don't see us," said LC.

At that moment Lulu kicked open the Critters' kitchen door.

"Aaahhh!!!!!" screamed Bunny and Little Sister.

But no one screamed louder than Lulu Creamcheese when she came face-to-face with two hundred boxes of Kernel Krunch cereal.

CHAPTER 8

HIDE-AND-SEEK

"Okay, you wormy little things," said Lulu. "Which box has the chip in it?"

"Chip?!" said Little Sister and Bunny, their eyes wide.

"Don't play dumb with me!" said Lulu. "If you don't give me that chip I'll . . ."

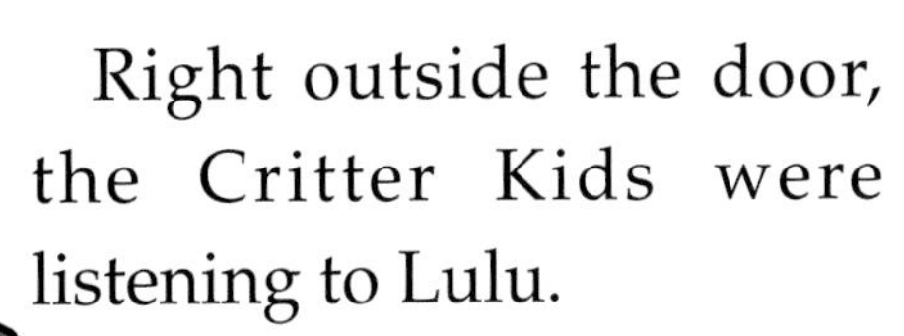

Right outside the door, the Critter Kids were listening to Lulu.

"They're after my dad's computer chip!" said LC. "We've got to stop them!"

Before LC could say anything else, they heard the sound of police sirens. Two police cars and one motorcycle pulled up in front of the Critters' house.

"That's the car, Officers," called Mrs. Crabtree, who was standing on her front porch. "The same one that put the dent in my shiny fender!"

Sergeant Pokey got off his motorcycle. The other officers got out of their cars.

"Hmmm," said Sergeant Pokey. "This car looks very familiar."

"They're at the Critters' house," said Mrs. Crabtree.

"Okay, follow me," said Sergeant Pokey to his squad.

Grandma had just finished her bath when Sergeant Pokey knocked on the door. She opened it and there, standing on the steps, were five police officers.

"Evening," said Sergeant Pokey. "We received a complaint from a Mrs. Crabtree about some critters who are visiting you. She claims they hit her car."

"Why, that's impossible," said Grandma. "Everyone here is too young to drive. See for yourself."

Grandma motioned the officers inside to the living room.

"Oh, my!" exclaimed Grandma. "Where is everyone?"

"We'll just check things out," said Sergeant Pokey as he and the officers moved toward the kitchen.

In the kitchen Lulu and Jellybean were tearing open box after box of Kernel Krunch cereal as fast as they could.

"Let's get out of here," said Jellybean.

"This place is crawling with fuzz."

"You haven't seen the end of me," said Lulu to Little Sister and Bunny. "I'll get that chip or my name isn't Lulu Creamcheese." She turned to Jellybean. "Grab as many boxes as you can and we'll make a run for it," she said.

Lulu and Jellybean ran out the back door, their arms filled with boxes of Kernel Krunch cereal.

"Now!" shouted LC to the Critter Kids as Lulu and Jellybean dashed outside. He, Tiger, and Henrietta held up one end of a garden hose while Gabby, Gator, and Velvet held up the other. Lulu and Jellybean tripped and fell over the hose.

Then LC ran to the side of the house and turned on the sprinkler system. Suddenly there was water everywhere.

Each time Lulu and Jellybean tried to stand up, they slipped on the wet grass and fell again.

When Mr. and Mrs. Critter turned down Green Frog Lane, they were shocked to see police cars surrounding their house.

"Oh, no!" said Mrs. Critter. "I told you something was wrong."

Mr. Critter pulled up in front of the house and they both jumped out of the car.

"What's going on?" asked Mr. Critter, running toward the crowd outside his house.

"That's exactly what I'm trying to find out," said Sergeant Pokey.

"Jellybean, what are you doing here?" asked Mr. Critter.

"You know him?" asked Sergeant Pokey.

"Yes," said Mr. Critter. "He's our new mailcritter at Coconut Computers."

"They were trying to steal your chip, Dad," said LC.

"So it was an inside job," said Gabby.

"What?" asked Mr. Critter.

"It all started when I got this strange E-mail message at school about Kernel Krunch," said LC.

"School!" said Lulu. "What was my message doing at your school?"

"You told me to send the E-mail to LC," said Jellybean.

"Not that LC," screamed Lulu.

"So that's what happened," said Gabby. "Her initials are LC, too. You got her E-mail by mistake."

"You pea brain!" Lulu yelled at Jellybean. "You were only supposed to send the message about Kernel Krunch to one classified address—mine!"

"Kernel Krunch," said Mr. Critter. "That's the name of my new chip. It's worth millions."

"That's right," said Lulu. "And that chip was supposed to be mine!"

"Well, we're going to take these two downtown," said Sergeant Pokey as he handcuffed Lulu and Jellybean. "These kids did a great job of capturing these computer criminals!" He and the other officers led Lulu and Jellybean away.

"But where's my chip now?" asked Mr. Critter.

"Oh, don't worry, dear," said Grandma. "It's in the kitchen in the Kernel Krunch cereal box."

"Uh-oh," whispered Little Sister to Bunny. "I'm in big trouble now."

Everybody went into the kitchen.

"Which box?!" gasped Mr. Critter.

"Where did all this cereal come from?" asked Grandma.

"I ordered it from the market," said Little Sister, staring at the ground.

"You what?!" said Mr. Critter. "You're going to be in big trouble for this."

"But, Dad," said LC. "If it wasn't for Little Sister ordering all these boxes of cereal, Lulu and Jellybean would have stolen your chip."

"They couldn't find the chip because they didn't know which box of cereal it was in," explained Gabby.

"This is so confusing," said Mrs. Critter.

"Yeah," said Henrietta. "I can't think when I'm hungry. Can I have some of this Kernel Krunch cereal?"

"Sure," said Mr. Critter, reaching for a box of cereal. "Everybody can have some cereal. We've got to eat our way through all these boxes till we find my chip."

"Dad, you know what?" said LC, tearing open a box of Kernel Krunch cereal. "If we're really lucky, we might even find the Super Snazzy Krunchometer Watch . . ."